NOT SO SMALL

Written by
Pat Zietlow Miller

Illustrated by
Paola Escobar

Quill Tree Books
An Imprint of HarperCollinsPublishers

3994011

Quill Tree Books is an imprint of HarperCollins Publishers.

Not So Small
Text copyright © 2022 by Patricia Miller
Illustrations copyright © 2022 by Paola Escobar
All rights reserved. Manufactured in Italy.

Library of Congress Control Number: 2021933232
ISBN 978-0-06-284744-7

The artist used Adobe Photoshop to create the digital illustrations for this book.
Typography by Rachel Zegar
22 23 24 25 26   RTLO   10 9 8 7 6 5 4 3 2 1
❖
First Edition

To Jeff Witthuhn—for being fierce
—P.Z.M.

For those who even feeling small have had
the courage to raise and share their voice
—P.E.

Big things get noticed.

Tall buildings.
Loud voices.
Wide walls.

Next to them, some people feel small.

Like puffs of dandelion fuzz.
Not needed.
Or known.
Barely seen.

But remember . . .

One acorn grows an oak.

One pebble sends out ripples.

One snowflake starts a storm.

And dandelion fuzz can
cause a BIG SNEEZE.

One person can get noticed
even if they feel small.

By talking to one friend.   Or four.

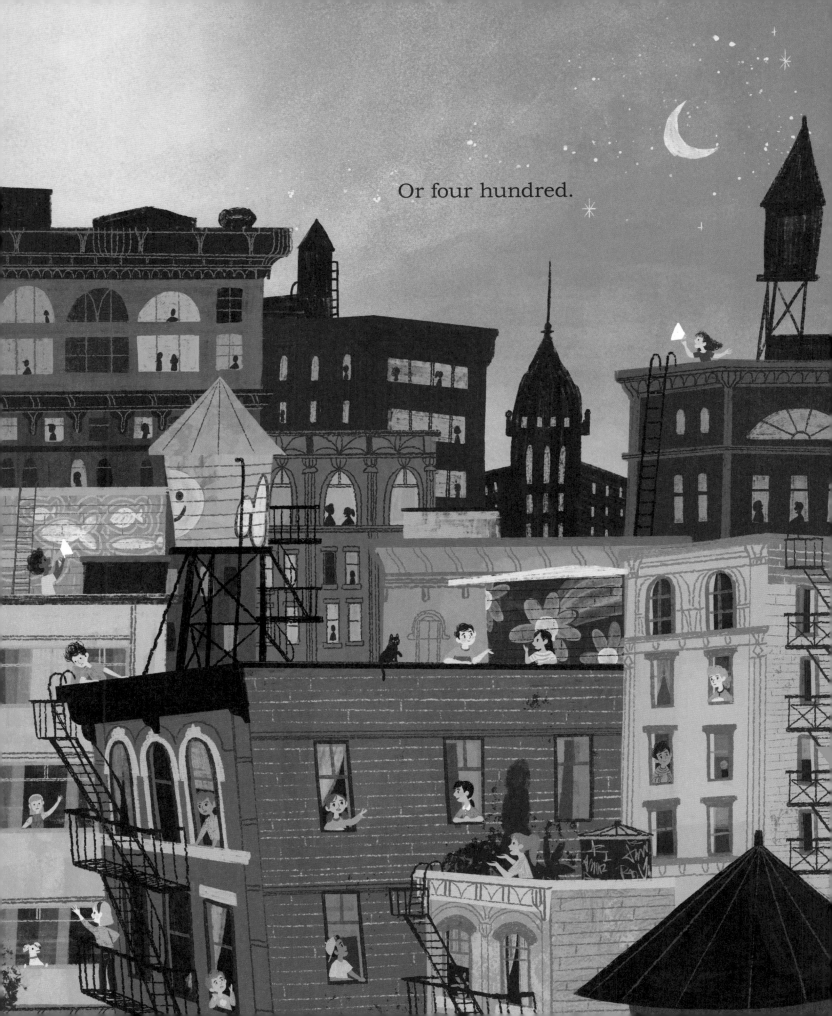

Or four hundred.

By writing.

Postcards.

Letters.

Or articles.

By walking.

In their neighborhood.

Around their city.

To their capitol.

Because . . .

A small voice can travel for miles.
Showing kindness.
Hope.
And love.

A small pencil can write big words.

Like *equality*.

Responsibility.

And *compassion*.

A small step can bring you closer.
To friendship.
Truth.
And fairness.

As those talkers, writers, and walkers
spread the word, some become more. And more
become many.

Just like dandelions.

Until . . .

Their voices form a chorus.

Their lines turn into signs.

And their steps
become so strong they
cannot be ignored.

One person can do something worth noticing.

By persisting.

One person can make a
mark when it matters most.

And inspire others to do
the same.

And then . . .

Then . . .

Together

Despite the bigness that surrounds them,
no one feels small.

At all.